*For all parents and kids
who share music with each other*
—R. C.

*For Ivy, Ralph's number one fan,
right here in my very own house*
—C. M. H.

Henry Holt and Company, LLC
Publishers since 1866
175 Fifth Avenue
New York, New York 10010
www.HenryHoltKids.com

Henry Holt® is a registered trademark of Henry Holt and Company, LLC.
Compilation copyright © 2008 by Ralph Covert
Illustrations copyright © 2008 by Charise Mericle Harper
All songs © Waterdog Music (ASCAP) except
"Happy Lemons" copyright © Waterdog Music/Tiger Tom Tunes (ASCAP)
All photographs of Ralph Covert © Peter Thompson, © Waterdog Music
All rights reserved.
Distributed in Canada by H. B. Fenn and Company Ltd.

Library of Congress Cataloging-in-Publication Data
Covert, Ralph.
Ralph's world rocks! / by Ralph Covert ; illustrations by Charise Mericle Harper.—1st ed.
p. cm.
ISBN-13: 978-0-8050-8735-2
ISBN-10: 0-8050-8735-4
1. Children's songs—Texts.
I. Harper, Charise Mericle. ill II. Title.
M1992.C68 2008   782.42164'0268—dc22   2007041955

First edition—2008
Book design by Lauren Lihn
The artist used acrylic paints and collage on illustration board to create the illustrations for this book.
Printed in China on acid-free paper. ∞

1 3 5 7 9 10 8 6 4 2

Ralph's World Rocks!

words and music by
Ralph Covert

Illustrations by
Charise Mericle Harper

HENRY HOLT AND COMPANY • NEW YORK

Contents

A Note from Ralph

As a child, I spent many hours in the magical places I could visit in my imagination. Some of my happiest memories are about being lost in a good book, swept away by a favorite song, or exploring a world I'd created with toys, in the sandbox, or with my friends. It's a happy irony that I've grown up to be able to share those places with others through my songs.

There came a point in my youth when I reached a fork in the road. I've always loved both making music and writing stories, and had dreamed equally of being a musician and an author. I chose the path of music at that time and lived my dream with my rock band, The Bad Examples, and with Ralph's World. Later, with my friend G. Riley Mills, I explored playwriting and adapting some of those plays into books. With this collection of Ralph's World songs, the paths finally all come together—songs presented in a book, with illustrations by another one of my best friends, Charise Mericle Harper.

I'm looking forward to the next part of this magical journey— writing stories and making more books, singing and sharing more songs, and playing with my friends in the sandbox. Hmmm. . . . The books and songs will probably keep me too busy to spend much time in the sandbox, but I'll definitely share the journey with my friends!

Who's the dog who makes the children giggle?
It's **Monster**.
Who's the dog who's fluffy as a pillow? . . .
   It's **Monster**!
Who's the dog who barks so loud she scared
   the shadow from the cloud?
It's **Monster** . . . **Monster**!

Who's the fastest puppy at the park?
It's **Monster**.
She's got a special hug for every pup. . . .
   It's **Monster**!
Who's the dog who chased the cat so fast
   the cat was at her back?
It's **Monster** . . . **Monster**!

Who's the softest snuggler on the couch?
It's **Monster**.
Who's the wettest kisser on the mouth? . . .
   It's **Monster**!
Waiting there at the pound, so happy that
   she was found.

M . . . O . . . N . . . S . . . T . . . E . . . R.
(She's a canine superstar!)
Here comes Monster back again—
R . . . E . . . T . . . S . . . N . . . O . . . M.

Who's the dog whose paws are always clean?
It's **Monster**.
Who's the hippest terrier on the scene? . . .
   It's **Monster**!
Who's so sweet they let her sit on the front desk
   at the vet?
It's **Monster** . . . **Monster**!

We Are Ants

We are ants, ants in your pants,
Ants in the kitchen, ants who love to dance.
Ants who sing and go to the moon.
Why are we marching? We are ants!

Gimme gimme gimme gimme gimme gimme
    gimme gimme something sweet—
We love sugar, we love candy!
Gimme gimme gimme gimme gimme gimme
    gimme gimme something sweet to eat—
We love chocolate, we love honey!

We are ants, and uncles of our ants.
Our mother's a queen, so her sister's our aunt.
Our brothers are ants, but so is our dad!
Why are we marching? We are ants!

Gimme gimme gimme gimme gimme gimme
    gimme gimme something sweet—
We love sugar, we love candy!
Gimme gimme gimme gimme gimme gimme
    gimme gimme something sweet to eat—
We love chocolate, we love honey!

We're black ants and red ants, too,
Ants at a picnic and ants at the zoo.
Ants who crawl inside of your pants.
Why are we marching? **WE ARE ANTS!**

11

Freddy Bear the Teddy Bear

There was a teddy bear named Freddy Bear
Who lives on top of a mountain made of
    chocolate cake.
He says, "I want my friends to come sing and
    dance with me,
We'll put on our pajamas, have a hootenanny."

Well, my right hand is all the boys I know.
And my left hand is all the girls I know.
When you put 'em all together they make
    a happy sound—
(Clap clap clap clap—clap clap clap clap)
That's the way the world goes round . . .

With a teddy bear named Freddy Bear
Who lives on top of a mountain made of
    chocolate cake.
He says, "I want my friends to come sing and
    dance with me,
We'll put on our pajamas, have a hootenanny."

Well, my right cheek is where my mommy kisses me,
And my left cheek is where my daddy kisses me.
When they kiss me all together it makes
    a happy sound—
(Kiss kiss kiss kiss— kiss kiss kiss kiss)
That's the way the world goes round . . .

With a teddy bear named Freddy Bear
Who lives on top of a mountain made of
CHOCOLATE CAKE!

BOYS

GIRLS

Harry's Haunted Halloween Circus

Harry's Haunted Halloween Circus,
It's Harry's Haunted Halloween Circus.
There's ghosts that sting, goblins with wings,
Very many scary things
In Harry's Haunted Halloween Circus!

Have you seen the phantom acrobat
Fly through the air without a net?
(We all knew him.)
The juggler throws his balls so high
And then they fall down from the sky . . .
     right through him.

In Harry's Haunted Halloween Circus,
Harry's Haunted Halloween Circus!

Have you seen the ghosts of circus past
Reach out from haunted circus tents?
(So tragic!)
Have you seen the brokenhearted clown?
And all the strong men falling down?
(Well, have you?)

In Harry's Haunted Halloween Circus,
It's Harry's Haunted Halloween Circus.
There's ghosts that sting, goblins with wings,
Very many scary things
In Harry's Haunted Halloween Circus.

LEMONADE

lemonade

Happy Lemons

Happy lemons for happy days,
Happy people with smiling faces,
Happiness is a glass of lemonade.

Lemonade, in the shade—
Everyone loves lemonade.

La la la la la la la la La la la la la la la la la la la la la la la la la la la la **lemonade**!

LEMONADE

Dump Truck

Well, I'm working, working all day in my dump truck.

Oh, I'm working, working all day in my dump truck.

I got a steam shovel, dig the dirt away, it goes *toot-toot*.

I got a steam shovel, dig the dirt away,

And I keep on digging down—dig my hole in the ground—
DUMP TRUCK!

Well, I'm digging, digging lots of dirt with my backhoe.

Oh, I'm digging, digging lots of dirt with my backhoe.

I got an earthmover, scrape the dirt away, it goes *toot-toot*.

I got an earthmover, scrape the dirt away,

And I keep on digging down—dig my hole in the ground—
DUMP TRUCK!

I dig down, I dig down into the ground,

I'm a miner, I'm a miner '49er.

Dig my hole down to Pittsburgh or maybe China—
DUMP TRUCK!

Well, I'm digging, digging lots of dirt into my  !
Well, I'm digging, digging lots of dirt into my !
I got a steam shovel, dig the dirt away, it goes *toot-toot*.
I got a steam shovel, dig the dirt away,
And I keep on digging down—dig my hole in the ground—
DUMP TRUCK!

Peggy's Pie Parlor Polka

When I want a piece of pie,
    I polka down to Peggy's,
I know I'm a very hungry guy, so I say,
    "May I please have a slice?"
And if I want some chocolate meringue,
    I run back in like a boomerang,
And in the sun or in the rain,
    I do the **Peggy's Pie Parlor Polka.**

Raspberry, strawberry, lemon-lime—
    summertime feels so fine,
If you want pie of any kind,
    polka down to Peggy's Pie Parlor.

I love an apple pie (it loves me . . .).
I love pumpkin, pecan (oh, how lovely . . .).
I love Peggy, and she loves me.
(At least she gives me pie to eat!)

Raspberry, strawberry, lemon-lime—
    summertime feels so fine,
If you want pie of any kind,
    polka down to Peggy's Pie Parlor.

Emily Miller

Emily Miller has fur on her belly
And nobody seems to be worried.
Emily Miller is bouncing
    and pouncing
And leaping about in a hurry.

She climbs on the table
    and jumps to the sofa.
She's running all over the house.
She sits in the window
    and won't go to school.
She's trying to play with a mouse!

Well, what would her mother say?
What would her mother say?
What would she say about that?

What would her mother say?
What would her mother say?
Emily Miller's a . . .

Meow!

Do the Math

Tony saw three sides to everything,
The good, the bad, and what was
   in between.
He was always very stable,
Your basic blue triangle.

His best friend was Sanderson
   the Square,
Sandy to his friends, with sandy hair.
He always wore red-checkered socks
And always thought inside the box.

So different from each other,
Different shapes and different colors.
But friends are friends,
   so do the math.

They both liked to play with
   Larry Line,
He was a real straight kind of guy.
He liked to draw from dot to dot.
And they all played that game a lot.

There was a new girl in their class,
Polly Hedron, a non-Euclidean lass.
Even though she broke the rules
They all found her pretty cool.

They were best friends,
   so do the math.
They all had fun, so do the math.
1 + 1 + 1 + 1!

Everybody went to the preschool fair.
People of every shape were there.
They did the boogie and they did
   the stomp,
They did the math till the sun
   came up.

Do the math!
  Do the math!
    Do the math!

Larry the Line did the twist,
Said, "Betcha didn't know
   I could dance like this!"
Polly did the boogaloo
With Sanderson and Tony, too!

Do the math!
  Do the math!
    Do the math!

Grab your partner one more time
On the left side of the equal sign!
1 + 1 + 1 + 1!
Everybody was having fun!

EVERYBODY WENT TO THE PRESCHOOL FAIR

Surfin' in My Imagination

I wanna go surfin' in my imagination
'Cause I won't get to go on my vacation.
I'll come home from school in the afternoon,
I'm gonna hit the beach in my bedroom,
Surfin' in my imagination.

Okay, let's go surfin'!
Balance on your surfboards,
Bend your knees and stick out your arms!
Here comes a big wave—
    faster, faster, faster, faster—wipe out!

I wanna go surfin' in my imagination
'Cause I won't get to go on my vacation.
I'll come home from school in the afternoon,
I'm gonna hit the beach in my bedroom,
Surfin' in my imagination.

Okay, let's see if you can balance on
    one foot!
Yeah! Say "Yo, dude!"
Here comes a big wave—
    faster, faster, faster—wipe out!

Let the River Flow

I'm gonna float my raft down the Mississippi,
Down the Allegheny, down the Ohio.
I'm gonna float my raft down the Rio Grande,
And I'll let that river flow.

I'm gonna sail my boat across Lake Michigan,
Across Lake Erie, across Lake Tahoe.
I'm gonna sail my boat up the Hudson River . . .
And I'll let that river flow.

I'm going down down down down down
    the mighty river,
Down down down down,
Let the river flow.

I'm gonna sail my boat down the Missouri,
Across the Potomac, down the Kanawha.
I'm gonna sail my boat through
    the Delta Basin . . .
And I'll let that river flow.

I'm gonna sail my ship across the ocean,
Across the water of the Gulf of Mexico.
I'm gonna sail my ship up the Mississippi,
And let that river flow.

I'm going down down down down down
    the mighty river,
Down down down down,
Let the river flow.

Sunny Day, Rainy Day, Anytime Band

There's a *boom-boom-boom* in
    the living room,
The kids are **banging** on the drums,
A *boom-boom-boom* in the living room—
Everybody's having **fun**!

Well, they're **spinning** all around
    in the living room.
The kids are starting to **dance**,
They're **spinning** all around
    in the living room—
Playing in a rock-and-roll band!

It's the Sunny Day, Rainy Day,
    Anytime Band,
Everybody's **laughing**.
Sunny Day, Rainy Day, Anytime Band.

Well, they're **jumping** up and down
    in the living room,
The kids are **playing** the guitar,
Jumping up and down
    in the living room—
Who's gonna be a rock star?

It's the Sunny Day, Rainy Day,
    Anytime Band,
Everybody's **laughing**.
Sunny Day, Rainy Day, Anytime Band.
Everybody's **happy**.
Sunny Day, Rainy Day, Anytime Band!

BAND

Come play
and sing along!

Guitar chords used in the songs

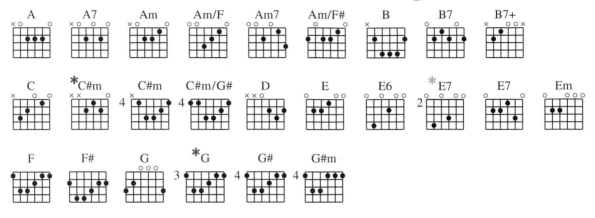

A   A7   Am   Am/F   Am7   Am/F#   B   B7   B7+

C   *C#m   C#m   C#m/G#   D   E   E6   *E7   E7   Em

F   F#   G   *G   G#   G#m

* Used in "Monster" only
* Used in "Surfin' in My Imagination" only
* Used in "Sunny Day, Rainy Day, Anytime Band" only

Monster

[verse 1]

E   D
Who's the dog who makes the children
    A
    giggle?
B
It's Monster.
E   D   A
Who's the dog who's fluffy as a pillow? . . .
        B
        It's Monster!
G#m   C#m   A
Who's the dog who barks so loud she scared
            F#
    the shadow from the cloud?
    E   B7+   A   B
It's Monster . . . Monster!
    E   B7+   A   B
    Monster . . . Monster!

[verse 2]

E   D   A
Who's the fastest puppy at the park?
    B
It's Monster.
E   D   A
She's got a special hug for every pup. . . .
        B
        It's Monster!
G#m   C#m
Who's the dog who chased the cat
    A   F#
    so fast the cat was at her back?
    E   B7+   A   B
It's Monster . . . Monster!
    E   B7+   A   B
    Monster . . . Monster!

[verse 3]

E   D   A
Who's the softest snuggler on the couch?
    B
It's Monster.
E   D   A
Who's the wettest kisser on the mouth? . . .
        B
        It's Monster!
G#m   C#m
Waiting there at the pound,
    A   F#
    so happy that she was found.
Em   B7
M . . . O . . . N . . . S . . . T . . . E . . . R.
B7   Em
(She's a canine superstar!)
Em   Am
Here comes Monster back again—
B7
R . . . E . . . T . . . S . . . N . . . O . . . M.

[verse 4]

E   D   A
Who's the dog whose paws are always clean?
    B
It's Monster.
E   D   A
Who's the hippest terrier on the scene? . . .
        B
        It's Monster.
G#m   C#m
Who's so sweet they let her sit
    A   F#
    on the front desk at the vet?
E   B7+   A   B
It's Monster . . . Monster! (repeat 3 times)

We Are Ants

[verse 1]

C   Am   F   G
We are ants, ants in your pants,
C   F   G
Ants in the kitchen, ants who love to dance.
C   Am   F   G
Ants who sing and go to the moon.
C   Am   [no chord]
Why are we marching? We are ants!

[chorus]

G   Em
Gimme gimme gimme gimme gimme
             C
gimme gimme gimme
        D
something sweet—
G   Em   C   D
We love sugar, we love candy!
G   Em
Gimme gimme gimme gimme gimme
                C
gimme gimme gimme something sweet
     D
to eat—
G   Em   C   D
We love chocolate, we love honey!

[verse 2]

C   Am   F   G
We are ants, and uncles of our ants.
C   Am   F
Our mother's a queen, so her sister's our
    G
aunt.
C   Am   F   G
Our brothers are ants, but so is our dad!
C   Am   [no chord]
Why are we marching? We are ants!

[chorus]

[verse 3]

C   Am   F   G
We're black ants and red ants, too,
C   Am   F   G
Ants at a picnic and at the zoo.
C   Am   F   G
Ants who crawl inside of your pants,
C   Am   [no chord]
Why are we marching? WE ARE ANTS!

Freddy Bear the Teddy Bear

[chorus]

               A
There was a teddy bear named Freddy Bear
     E
Who lives on top of a mountain made of
     A
   chocolate cake.
          A
He says, "I want my friends to come sing and
    dance with me,
 E   A
We'll put on our pajamas, have a hootenanny."

[verse 1]

       A
Well, my right hand is all the boys I know.
        E   A
And my left hand is all the girls I know.
          A
When you put 'em all together they make
   a happy sound—
[no chord]
[Clap clap clap clap—clap clap clap clap]
               E
That's the way the world goes round with a
[return to chorus and drop "With a"]
Teddy bear named Freddy Bear
     E   A
Who lives on top of a mountain made of
   chocolate cake.
He says, "I want my friends to come sing and
   dance with me,
 E   A
We'll put on our pajamas, have a hootenanny."

[verse 2]

     A
Well, my right cheek is where my mommy
   kisses me,
              E
And my left cheek is where my daddy
 A
   kisses me.
        A
When they kiss me all together it makes a
   happy sound—
[no chord]
[Kiss kiss kiss kiss—kiss kiss kiss kiss]
               E
That's the way the world goes round with a
Teddy bear named Freddy Bear
     E   A
Who lives on top of a mountain made of
   CHOCOLATE CAKE!

Harry's Haunted Halloween Circus

[INTRO: Am Am/F Am/F# Am/F D F—repeat twice]

[chorus]

Am   G   D
Harry's Haunted Halloween Circus,
Am   G   D
It's Harry's Haunted Halloween Circus.
Am   G
There's ghosts that sting, goblins with wings,
D   F
Very many scary things
      Am   G   D
In Harry's Haunted Halloween Circus!

[verse 1]

Am   E
Have you seen the phantom acrobat
                   G
Fly through the air without a net?
          D
(We all knew him.)
Am   E
The juggler throws his balls so high
[E]   G
And then they fall down from the sky . . .
       D
   right through him.

[INTRO CHORDS]

      AM   G   D
In Harry's Haunted Halloween Circus,
Am   G   D
Harry's Haunted Halloween Circus!

[verse 2]
Am
Have you seen the ghosts of circus past
E   G
Reach out from haunted circus tents?
       D
(So tragic!)
Am   E
Have you seen the brokenhearted clown?
                   G
And all the strong men falling down?
     D
(Well, have you?)

[chorus]

[INTRO CHORDS]

      Am   G   D
In Harry's Haunted Halloween Circus,
      Am   G   D
It's Harry's Haunted Halloween Circus.
          Am   G
There's ghosts that sting, goblins with wings
D   F
Very many scary things
      Am   G   D
In Harry's Haunted Halloween Circus.

Dump Truck

           A7
Well, I'm working, working all day in my

   dump truck.
              A7
Oh, I'm working, working all day in my
     D7
   dump truck.
I got a steam shovel, dig the dirt away,
        D7
   it goes *toot-toot.*
          E7
I got a steam shovel, dig the dirt away,
                A7
And I keep on digging down—dig my hole
      A7
   in the ground—DUMP TRUCK!

Well, I'm digging, digging lots of dirt with
        A7
   my backhoe.
Oh, I'm digging, digging lots of dirt with my
       D7
   backhoe.
I got an earthmover, scrape the dirt away,
        D7
   it goes *toot-toot.*
          E7
I got an earthmover, scrape the dirt away,
                A7
And I keep on digging down—dig my hole
D   G   A7
   in the ground—DUMP TRUCK!
D   G   A7
I dig down, I dig down into the ground,
D   G   A7
I'm a miner, I'm a miner '49er.
              A7
Dig my hole down to Pittsburgh or maybe
       A7
   China—DUMP TRUCK!

Well, I'm digging, digging lots of dirt into
        A7
   my (dump truck).

Well, I'm digging, digging lots of dirt into
        D7
   my (dump truck).
I got a steam shovel, dig the dirt away,
        D7
   it goes *toot-toot.*
        D7
I got a steam shovel, dig the dirt away,
               A7
And I keep on digging down—dig my hole

   in the ground—DUMP TRUCK!

Peggy's Pie Parlor Polka

[INTRO: A A E A (repeat twice)
B B F# B (repeat twice)]

[chorus 1]

A   E
When I want a piece of pie, I polka down
 A
  to Peggy's,
(A)   E
I know I'm a very hungry guy, so I say,
   A
  "May I please have a slice?"
(A)
And if I want some chocolate meringue,
  E   A
  I run back in like a boomerang,
    (A)
And in the sun or in the rain, I do the
 E   A
  Peggy's Pie Parlor Polka.

A A E A [repeat twice]
B B F# B [repeat twice]

[verse]

A
Raspberry, strawberry, lemon-lime—
  E   A
  summertime feels so fine,
(A)   E
If you want pie of any kind, polka down
     E
  to Peggy's Pie Parlor.
      D (D A D)
I love an apple pie (it loves me . . .).
A
I love pumpkin, pecan (oh, how lovely . . .).
D
I love Peggy, and she loves me.
  B7   E7
(At least she gives me pie to eat!)

[repeat half of verse]

[chorus 2]

A   E
When I want a piece of pie, I polka down
 A
  to Peggy's,
(A)   E
I know I'm a very hungry guy, so I say,
   A E A
  "May I please have a slice?"
A   E
And if I want some chocolate meringue,
  A
  I run back in like a boomerang,
(A)
And in the sun or in the rain, I do the
 E   A   E
  Peggy's Pie Parlor Polka,
  E   A   E
The Peggy's Pie Parlor Polka,
 E   A   E
I do the Peggy's Pie Parlor Polka!

Emily Miller

D
Emily Miller has fur on her belly

And nobody seems to be worried.

Emily Miller is bouncing and pouncing

And leaping about in a hurry.

         G   D
She climbs on the table and jumps to the sofa.
  A   D
She's running all over the house.

She sits in the window and won't go to school.
    E   A
She's trying to play with a mouse!
    G
Well, what would her mother say?
D
What would her mother say?
A   D
What would she say about that?
G
What would her mother say?
D
What would her mother say?
A   (D)
Emily Miller's a . . .

Meow!

Happy Lemons

[verse]
G
Happy lemons for happy days,
D
Happy people with smiling faces,
C   G
Happiness is a glass of lemonade.

[repeat verse]

[chorus]
G   C G   D
Lemonade, in the shade—
G   C   GD G
Everyone loves lemonade.

[repeat verse and repeat chorus twice]
G
La la la la la la la la la
C
La la la la la la la la la
G   D
La la la la la la la la lemonade
G
La la la la la la la la la
C
La la la la la la la la la
Am   D
La la la la la la la la lemonade.

[repeat chorus and verse]

(end La la's)

G C Am D

G C G D

G C G D

G C Am D

Do the Math

[verse 1]

A   A   G   A   G A G
Tony saw three sides to everything,

     A   G   A
The good, the bad, and what was

      G   A   G A G
   in between.

A   G   A   G
He was always very stable,

D   E   A G A G
Your basic blue triangle.

[verse 2]

A   G   A   G
His best friend was Sanderson

       A   G A G
   the Square,

A   G   A   G   A   G A G
Sandy to his friends, with sandy hair.

A   G   A   G
He always wore red-checkered socks

D   E   A G A G
And always thought inside the box.

[chorus]

D   E
So different from each other,

G   A
Different shapes and different colors.

D   C   G   A   G A G
But friends are friends, so do the math.

[verse 3]

A   G   A
They both liked to play with

   G   A   G A G
   Larry Line,

A   G   A   G   A   G A G
He was a real straight kind of guy.

A   G   A   G
He liked to draw from dot to dot.

     D   E   A G A G
And they all played that game a lot.

[chorus]

[verse 4]

A   G   A   G   A   G A G
There was a new girl in their class,

A   G   A   G   A G A G
Polly Hedron, a non-Euclidean lass.

A   G   A   G
Even though she broke the rules

D   E
They all found her pretty cool.

D   C   G   D
They were best friends, so do the math.

(D)   C   G   D
They all had fun, so do the math.

(D)   C   A
1 + 1 + 1 + 1!

[no chords]

Everybody went to the preschool fair.

People of every shape were there.

They did the boogie and they did the stomp,

They did the math till the sun came up.

[outro chorus]

        B   F#
Do the math!

        A   E
Do the math!

Larry the Line did the twist,

Said, "Betcha didn't know I could dance

   like this!"

Polly did the boogaloo

With Sanderson and Tony, too!

[Outro chorus]

Grab your partner one more time

On the left side of the equal sign!

1 + 1 + 1 + 1!

Everybody was having fun!

Surfin' in My Imagination

[chorus]

             E   A
I wanna go surfin' in my imagination

E   B7
'Cause I won't get to go on my vacation.

               E
I'll come home from school in the afternoon,

             A
I'm gonna hit the beach in my bedroom,

E   B7   E
Surfin' in my imagination.

[slide finger down E string, surf riff E-G on bass (E string),
then A-C string (A string)]

E
Okay, let's go surfin'!

Balance on your surfboards,

A   E
Bend your knees and stick out your arms!

                             F F#   G
Here comes a big wave—faster, faster, faster,

       G#
   faster—wipe out!

[chorus]

E
Okay, let's see if you can balance on one foot!

            A   E
Yeah! Say "Yo, dude!"

                       F   F#
Here comes a big wave—faster, faster,

      G
   faster—wipe out!

[chorus]

Let the River Flow

A   D   A
I'm gonna float my raft down the Mississippi,
    E   A
Down the Allegheny, down the Ohio.
(A)   D
I'm gonna float my raft down the
  A
 Rio Grande,
   E   A
And I'll let that river flow.
(A)   D
I'm gonna sail my boat across Lake
 A
 Michigan,
    E   A
Across Lake Erie across Lake Tahoe.
      D
I'm gonna sail my boat up the Hudson
 A
 River . . .
   E   A
And I'll let that river flow.

[chorus]
(A)   E   D
I'm going down down down down down
  A
 the mighty river,
(A)   E
Down down down down,
D   A
Let the river flow.

[repeat half of chorus]
A   D   A
I'm gonna sail my boat down the Missouri,
   E   A
Across the Potomac, down the Kanawha.
      D
I'm gonna sail my boat through the Delta
 A
 Basin . . .
   E   A
And I'll let that river flow.

[half chorus instrumental] D E F# B
           D E
A   D   A
I'm gonna sail my ship across the ocean,
   E   A
Across the water of the Gulf of Mexico.
    D   A
I'm gonna sail my ship up the Mississippi,
   E   A
And I'll let that river flow.

[chorus repeats twice]

Sunny Day, Rainy Day, Anytime Band

[Intro riff:]   E   E6   E7   E6

E   E6   E7   E6
There's a *boom-boom-boom* in the living room,
  E   E6   E7 E6
The kids are banging on the drums,
  E   E6   E7 E6
A *boom-boom-boom* in the living room—

[repeat intro riff twice]
G   D
Everybody's having fun!
   E   E6
Well, they're spinning all around in
   E7 E6
 the living room.
E6 E   E6 E7 E6
The kids are starting to dance,
     E   E6   E7
They're spinning all around in the living
   E6
 room—
G   D
Playing in a rock-and-roll band!

[intro riff once]
      G   D
It's the Sunny Day, Rainy Day, Anytime Band,
Am7
Everybody's laughing.
G   D
Sunny Day, Rainy Day, Anytime Band.

[repeat intro riff twice]
      E   E6
Well, they're jumping up and down in
   E7 E6
 the living room,
    E   E6   E7 E6
The kids are playing the guitar,
  E   E6   E7 E6
Jumping up and down in the living room—
G   D
Who's gonna be a rock star?

[intro riff once]
      G   D
It's the Sunny Day, Rainy Day, Anytime Band,
Am7
Everybody's laughing.
G   D
Sunny Day, Rainy Day, Anytime Band.
Am7
Everybody's happy.
G   D
Sunny Day, Rainy Day, Anytime Band!

[repeat intro riff twice]

[no chords through the next two lines]

Well, there's a *boom-boom-boom* in

 the living room,

The kids are banging on the drums,

A *boom-boom-boom* in the living room—
     G   D
Sunny Day, Rainy Day, Anytime Band,
Am7
Everybody's laughing.
G   D
Sunny Day, Rainy Day, Anytime Band,
Am7
Everybody's happy.
G   D
Sunny Day, Rainy Day, Anytime Band!

[repeat intro riff three times]

A *boom-boom-boom!* [repeat three times]